MAGGIE STERN

ACORN MAGIC

PICTURES BY
DONNA RUFF

Greenwillow Books, New York

Acrylic paints were used for the full-color art.
The text type is Leawood Medium BT.

Printed in Hong Kong by South China Printing Company (1988) Ltd.
First Edition   10   9   8   7   6   5   4   3   2   1

Library of Congress Cataloging-in-Publication Data
Stern, Maggie.
Acorn magic / by Maggie Stern ; pictures by Donna Ruff.
p.   cm.
Summary: Mrs. Potter takes Simon camping to look for birds,
but even though he brings along his magic acorn the trip
does not turn out the way he expected.
ISBN 0-688-15699-1
[1. Acorns—Fiction.   2. Bird watching—Fiction.
3. Camping—Fiction.]   I. Ruff, Donna, ill.
II. Title.   PZ7.S83875Ac   1998   [E]—dc21
97-36298   CIP   AC

For my mother
—M. S.

For my own little boy
—D. R.

It was Mrs. Potter who gave Simon the acorn.
The next day Simon spotted a scarlet bird with
black wings.

Mrs. Potter, who knew almost everything about
birds, told him that seeing a scarlet tanager was
lucky.

Then a few days later he
saw an owl in his backyard.
Mrs. Potter said the acorn
must be magic.

One hot morning Mrs. Potter walked across her
yard to Simon's house. Simon was sitting on
the front steps, spinning his acorn like a top.
"Simon," said Mrs. Potter, "how would you like
to go camping with me? Someone spotted
a pileated woodpecker on Mount Hancock.
If we went, maybe we'd see one, too."

Simon turned to his mother. "Please, can I go? Please?"

"Are you sure about this, Hope?" said his mother.

"Of course I'm sure!" said Mrs. Potter. "We'll be back tomorrow by lunch."

"I want to go, too!" said Simon's younger brother, Jack.

"Maybe next year," said his mother. "When you're older."

"Don't worry, Jack. I'll find you something special," said Simon.

Simon packed his stuffed moose and his sleeping bag. He put his acorn safely in his pocket.

Jack waved good-bye.

In the car Simon said to Mrs. Potter, "I want to find more acorns like the one you gave me."

"Dearie, where we're going, there are plenty of white oak trees. There won't be any shortage of acorns."

"Great!" said Simon. "Then I know we'll see *lots* of birds and animals."

Good things happened when he was with Mrs. Potter.

Blue mountains rose high above the lake at the campground.

After Mrs. Potter had pitched the tent, Simon unrolled his sleeping bag. He laid down his moose and tucked the acorn under its antlers so he wouldn't lose it. He was sure he'd find other lucky acorns.

"Let's be on our way," said Mrs. Potter. "We've got a lot to explore."

Simon followed close behind Mrs. Potter. His binoculars thumped against his chest. As they were winding up a steep trail, he reached down to pick up an acorn.

"Careful where you step," said Mrs. Potter as something dark slithered away. "You almost stepped on a garter snake!"

"Where?"

"Gone," said Mrs. Potter.

Simon walked with his nose to the ground.
"Look at these, Mrs. Potter." Simon was stuffing
handfuls of acorns into his pocket. "I'm going
to see a million animals now."
"Maybe," said Mrs. Potter.

"Simon, look up," said Mrs. Potter softly as she
stared through her binoculars. "A bald eagle."
But by the time his binoculars
were in focus, all Simon could
see were twisted, dark branches.

When they were deep in the woods,
Mrs. Potter sat down on a large rock.
She scanned the trees with her
binoculars.

Simon's pockets were so full that acorns were spilling out. He scurried around the trail to retrieve them.

Suddenly there was a clattering noise.

"Quick. In that tree," said Mrs. Potter.

"There's a goldfinch."

Simon grabbed one more acorn,
then looked up. The noise had stopped.
The bird had flown off.

Back at the campsite by the lake Mrs. Potter helped
Simon try his hand at fishing.
He felt a nibble at the end of the line. But when
he reeled it in, all he had caught was somebody's
torn sock.

"I haven't seen one animal this whole day," Simon said.
He reached in his pockets. "These acorns are stupid.
They're not lucky at all."
He hurled the acorns as far away as he could. They lay
scattered on the rocks and sand at the water's edge.

That evening rain hammered on the tent.
Thunder boomed.
In his sleeping bag Simon clung to his moose.
He reached for his lucky acorn and rubbed its
smooth bottom with his thumb.
"We're safe in here, dearie," said Mrs. Potter.
She turned on her flashlight.
A large branch cracked nearby.
"It's a tornado," said Simon.
"No, it's a summer storm. Listen, you can hear
the thunder. It's overhead now. Soon it will
pass."
Simon cried quietly into his moose's antlers.

Mrs. Potter patted his sleeping bag. "There are many things that don't happen the way we plan. Weather is only one of them."

"But *you* always see everything!" said Simon.

"I didn't see the pileated woodpecker," said Mrs. Potter.

With the first morning light Simon reached for his acorn. He rubbed its knobby hat. "I'll be careful not to lose you," he said.

Simon slipped out of the tent and went down to the lake. He looked around. A duck with green feathers sailed by. Tree frogs chirped in the distance.
Simon smiled.

Then he heard
a rustling sound.
He turned around
quietly.
At the edge of the
lake stood a moose.
It was enormous.
Its legs were tall
and thin like stilts.
Its velvety antlers
seemed to spread
across the sky.
Simon stood
frozen.
The moose looked
straight at him.
Its eyes gleamed
in the morning
light. Then it turned
away and plunged
straight into the
lake.

Simon watched in awe as the moose swam
toward the far shore. Its head and antlers slowly
faded away.

Simon ran over to where the moose had stood.
Its huge hoofmarks were imprinted in the sand.
Next to a mound of discarded water lilies and
twigs were pieces of half-chewed acorns.

Simon picked up an acorn hat that was still
whole and pressed it
onto the tip of his finger.

Simon raced back to their tent.

"Mrs. Potter," he shouted. "They worked. The acorns I threw away worked. I know it!"

While they drank hot chocolate by the campfire, Simon told Mrs. Potter all about the moose.

"Wait till I tell Jack," he said.

In the car, on their way home, Simon looked at his acorn and his new acorn hat.

"Mrs. Potter," he asked, "do you think acorns are *really* magic?"

"Dearie, one small acorn can become a tree so tall you can scarcely see the top." She paused. "If that isn't magic, then I don't know what is."

When he got home,
Simon raced upstairs
into Jack's bedroom,
slipped the acorn
hat off his finger,
and placed it on
Jack's pillow.

Then Simon ran outside. He dug a hole at the
far side of the backyard. Taking the acorn from
his pocket, he felt its pointed tip and carefully
planted it.

Simon knew the acorn would take a long
time to grow into a tree.
But he also knew that at any moment
magic could happen.